TRIXIE'S SPECIAL GUESTS

A.M. LUZZADER

ILLUSTRATED BY
JOSHUA BOSTWICK

Published by Knowledge Forest Press
P.O. Box 6331
Logan, UT 84341

Ebook ISBN-13: 978-1-949078-75-6
Paperback ISBN-13: 978-1-949078-74-9

Cover design by Stefanie at Beetiful Book Covers (beetifulbookcovers.com)

Editing by Chadd VanZanten

Interior illustrations by Joshua Bostwick

Contents

Chapter One

There are many different varieties of dogs. Some varieties grow very large, like Great Danes and St. Bernards. Some dogs are nearly as big as ponies, but most will not let you ride them. Other dog varieties are very small, like the Chihuahua (pronounced "chuh-waa-wuh").

Different dogs have different-colored fur. Irish Setters have red fur, American Eskimo Dogs are white, Labrador Retrievers are black, and Poodles can have gold fur. There are hundreds and hundreds of kinds of dogs, each with its own appearance.

Trixie was a Shih Tzu (pronounced "sheed-zoo"). Shih Tzus are one of the smaller dogs. In fact, Trixie's human, an older lady named Violet, sometimes carried Trixie in her purse. Trixie enjoyed riding in the purse, with just her head and her front paws sticking out. For Trixie, riding in Violet's purse was a little like flying in an airplane.

Like all Shih Tzus, Trixie had large round eyes and a very short snout. Her fur was cream-colored and brown, though tufts of gray had started appearing as she got older.

All dogs may look different, but Trixie knew that all dogs were related to the old ancestors. That meant that all dogs were also related to each other.

The old ancestor dogs lived thousands and thousands of years ago. Trixie often wondered what they had looked like. Were they large? Was their fur long or short? Maybe back then, all dogs looked similar to wolves.

Dogs were sworn to protect humans. They promised to always guard the humans from danger. Trixie knew about this because her mother had told her about the old ancestors when Trixie was a puppy. Trixie's mother had been told about the ancestors by her mother, who had been told by her mother before that.

Dogs had been protecting humans and telling the stories of the old ancestors for thousands of years.

Many years ago, Trixie was a young mother dog, and her puppies still lived at home with her. While they were still young, Trixie gathered them around her so she could teach them about the old ancestors.

Trixie had four puppies. Buster was the energetic one of the bunch. He loved to jump and bark. Aggie was timid but very smart and thoughtful. Riley loved to take naps in the sun. The fourth puppy, Lucy, was cute and very small, even for a Shih Tzu.

It wasn't easy for Trixie to make her puppies listen. They were each doing their own things. Buster was chasing his own tail round and round. Riley was sleeping.

Trixie told him, "Buster! Stop chasing your tail!"

Buster said, "I'm not chasing my tail! I'm chasing Lucy's tail!"

"No, you are not," said Lucy. "My tail is here with me."

"Oh!" cried Buster. "I thought that was your tail, Lucy."

"Riley," said Trixie, "wake up, dear."

"I am awake," said Riley sleepily. "I'm just resting my eyes."

"Listen, puppies," said Trixie. "I want to tell you an amazing story."

At last they settled down and listened.

"Dogs have always been magica

"This you already know. Hundreds an

years ago, the old ancestors were powerfully magical and free. They had so much magic, that they decided to create a new place to live. It would be a magical place just for dogs, a place that had all the things that dogs love," said Trixie.

"Did it have lots of trees?" asked Buster with excitement.

"Yes," replied Trixie. "So many trees."

"And lakes?" asked Aggie.

"Yes," replied Trixie. "Big beautiful lakes full of cool water to swim and play in."

"And comfy dog beds?" asked Riley.

"Yes," replied Trixie. "The comfiest! The new magical place created by the old ancestors had all these things and more. It was a wonderfully magical place where the only things dogs had to do was play and take naps and chew on bones. They called it Pupadise, the paradise for dogs."

"Does that place *really* exist?" asked Lucy. "Where is it?"

"It does," said Trixie.

"It's not on Earth, and you must use dog magic to go to Pupadise. After the ancestors worked together to create Pupadise, they all started moving there."

Buster wrinkled his nose. "So why aren't we there?"

Trixie smiled. "As you know, dogs aren't the only magical creatures."

"Cats can do magic," said Riley. "They're just not very nice about it."

"Birds can do magic, too," said Lucy.

"Yes, that's true," said Trixie, "but there was another magical creature."

The puppies perked up and listened more closely.

"These creatures were very magical," said Trixie, "but they used their magic to make everyone else miserable. And so they were called the Miseries, and they still exist today. In fact, Miseries are a very unpleasant force in the world."

"Why do they want to make everyone miserable?" asked Lucy.

"We don't know for sure," Trixie replied. "We think it's because the Miseries themselves are miserable, and so they want to make everyone else miserable, too."

"That doesn't sound very nice," said Aggie.

"It's not," said Trixie. "Luckily, our dog ancestors knew about the ways of the Miseries. A Misery can't be seen unless you use magic. They are like grumpy ghosts that fly around looking to stir up trouble. But even though you might not see a Misery, you can feel it when you're being haunted by one. You'll feel irritated and grumpy. Everything will feel uncomfortable. It's an awful feeling."

"So," said Riley, "if I feel irritated and grumpy, it means I'm being haunted by one of these grumpy ghosts?"

"No," answered Trixie, "not always. It's normal to feel that way sometimes. But the Miseries make it worse. They thrive on the misery of others."

"Oooh," said Trixie's puppies.

"Also," said Trixie, "The magical power of the Miseries increases when poor choices are made. If you tell a lie or say something unkind, any Miseries who are nearby will grow more powerful. This means they can make us feel more miserable."

"That sounds scary," said Lucy.

"Yes, a little," said Trixie, "but, if we make good choices, the Miseries get *less* powerful."

"Are there any Miseries in the land of Pupadise?" asked Aggie.

"No, there are no Miseries in Pupadise," said Trixie. "Pupadise is a place that is safe for dogs, and Miseries can never go there."

"I don't understand," said Buster. "Why don't we all go to Pupadise?"

"Just listen," said Trixie. "Thousands of years ago, all the dogs were moving to Pupadise. But then they noticed that the Miseries were making all the humans on Earth even more miserable."

"So," said Riley, "why didn't the humans use their magic and create a land for themselves?"

"Humans don't have magic," said Trixie.

"What about the spark spell to make light?" asked Lucy. "That's an easy one!"

"Humans don't have magic, dear," repeated Trixie.

"Or the detect magic spell?" asked Aggie.

"Puppies," said Trixie, "you're not listening to me. There may be a few humans who know a little magic. Sadly, most of them don't know any magic at all. So, they couldn't create a happy and magical place for themselves. And they can't fight off the Miseries on Earth with magic spells."

"Oh, those poor humans," said Riley.

"Yes, they were all so miserable," said Trixie. "The humans were suffering—always feeling angry or grouchy or unhappy."

The puppies' eyes grew wide and worried as they listened.

"This is why the old ancestors did not move to the land of Pupadise," explained Trixie. "They saw the suffering of the humans and decided to stay here to help them."

"They didn't go to Pupadise?" asked Buster in surprise.

"No," said Trixie. "It was a choice they made, a vow they took. The ancestors promised they would help the humans fight back against the Miseries. This decision, which was a *good* choice, weakened the power the Miseries had over the humans. And we dogs have been helping the humans ever since."

"That's amazing!" said Aggie.

The puppies jumped up and wagged their tails.

"Go dogs!" said Buster.

"To show their thanks," Trixie said, "the humans brought the dogs into their homes. The humans have forgotten this. They think we are just fun pets. But in the old days, they gave the dogs food and shelter to show their thanks. The humans were thankful for the help. This is how dogs became the humans' best friends," said Trixie.

"Woof! Woof!" barked Riley happily. "So, the ancestors defeated the Miseries?"

"No," replied Trixie. "That wasn't the end of the Miseries. They got so angry! The ancestors ruined their plans! And so they have been trying to torment the humans ever since. The Miseries wait for bad choices to be made, then they use their bad magic to tease and bother the humans. When you puppies get old enough, you can join the fight against the

Miseries. Will you use your magic to help protect the humans from the Miseries?"

"I will! I will!" yipped Lucy.

"Me too!" barked Aggie.

"I will!" cried Riley.

"Miseries, you better look out," said Buster, biting a toy rope and shaking it. "I'm going to get you!"

Trixie smiled. She was glad that her puppies would continue the tradition of the ancestors by using magic to protect humans from the Miseries.

"It's a responsibility you must carry out every day," said Trixie. "Always be on the look-out for a Misery. They can appear anywhere and any time."

"How can we know when they're around?" asked Aggie.

"They smell awful!" replied Trixie.

"What do they smell like?" asked Lucy.

"The worst thing you have ever smelled," said Trixie. "You'll know it when you smell it. You must always be aware of your surroundings and sniffing out the Miseries. Our sense of smell is the greatest tool we have to find the Miseries. The humans, sadly, cannot smell them."

There were other clues to find the Miseries, of

course. The trouble the Miseries caused, for example. Anytime a human was feeling grumpy or annoyed, it might be a sign that there was a Misery in the area.

A human might say, "I'm in a bad mood!" But they did not know that it might be a Misery.

But Trixie would know it was the work of a Misery. And when humans made poor choices, the worse it got.

Not every dog chose to keep the promise of the old ancestors to protect the humans. Some laughed at it and called it a silly old legend. Some very bad dogs even helped the Miseries. But Trixie, and most dogs, loved humans and wanted to help them, just like the dogs in the old days.

Since that time, dogs had improved their magic. But so had the Miseries. Trixie promised herself that she would always stand up against the Miseries.

"But what about Pupadise?" asked Riley. "Is it real? Does it really exist? Can we go there?"

"Yes, it's real," said Trixie. "We could go there, but I never have. This is my home and these humans are my family, just like you are."

This conversation with the puppies, Buster, Lily, Aggie, and Riley, had taken place many, many years ago. Trixie's puppies had grown up and gone to live with other human families, but Trixie was happy to know they were carrying on the tradition of the old ancestors—protecting their humans from the Miseries.

Trixie was an old dog now and so was her human, Violet. Violet's children had also grown up and moved away, and her husband Ollie had passed away. Now it was just Trixie and Violet. They lived together.

Trixie had done a good job at protecting her human family from the Miseries. She rarely saw any Miseries in their home. Because of this, Trixie had decided to become a teacher to the younger dogs in the neighborhood. She taught them about magic and the tricks of the Miseries.

Still, in her old age, Trixie had less energy. Instead of hunting out and fighting Miseries around the neighborhood, she spent most of her days napping.

Also, Trixie's senses weren't as sharp as they used to be. She couldn't see far away anymore. When she read from her spell book, she had to use eyeglasses. Her hearing wasn't as sharp as it once had been. Even her sense of smell wasn't as good as it used to be.

However, Trixie was still committed to fighting the Miseries.

I may be getting old, Trixie thought, *but those Miseries better not mess with me or my humans!*

Chapter Two

It was an exciting day for Trixie and Violet. Every morning, Violet put Trixie's leash onto her collar, and they took a walk together. Like Trixie, Violet was getting older. Her hair had turned white and her back was a bit stooped. She wore glasses, and she didn't walk very quickly anymore.

Trixie didn't mind. She loved seeing the neighborhood. Trixie loved to see the yards and houses and their neighbors. Two dogs that Trixie was helping to learn magic lived nearby. Trixie gave them a friendly bark as she and Violet passed by on the sidewalk.

The morning walk was supposed to be fun. However, Trixie still tried to sniff out Miseries lurking around the neighborhood. As they strolled along, Trixie sniffed the air and snuffled the ground for any hint of Miseries.

On that day, Trixie hoped there'd be nothing to investigate. That's because it was a special day for Trixie and Violet. Violet's son, Mark, and his family were coming to visit. Mark and his wife, Julie, had two children. Their names were Emily and Davis. They were Violet's grandchildren, and she loved them almost more than anything.

Trixie herself was fond of Emily and Davis, too. Emily was eight years old. She had bright blue eyes and long, golden hair. She liked singing, dancing, and reading books. When Emily visited Violet and Trixie, she'd often find a quiet spot in Violet's garden and would read a book. Trixie thought this was very pleasant. Trixie would sometimes join Emily in the garden and watch over her.

Davis was ten years old. He had shaggy brown hair and brown eyes. He liked to play football and baseball. When he visited, he would ask someone, anyone, to go outside and play catch. Any ball would do. If no baseball or football could be found, Davis was happy to throw an old torn-up tennis ball or even one of Trixie's play toys. If no one would throw a ball with Davis, he'd throw the ball to himself. Trixie loved playing with Davis, though she didn't run as fast or catch as well as she did when she was young.

As Trixie and Violet came around the block, they spotted the family's car. Trixie pulled on her leash, wanting to run, even though she wasn't very fast. Then she saw Davis and Emily.

"Trixie!" yelled Davis as he climbed out of the car.

Mark and Julie began to unload their suitcases from the car. Davis rushed over to unclip Trixie's leash and pick her up. Trixie happily licked his face.

These were Violet's grandchildren, but they reminded Trixie of her own puppies. She thought of Emily and Davis as her grandchildren, too.

"Hiya, girl!" said Emily, patting Trixie on the head. Trixie smiled.

"Oh, it's so good to see you!" Violet said, wrapping each member of the family with a big hug.

The kids' dad, Mark, picked up a big suitcase. "It was a long drive," he said.

"I've made up a room for the kids with a bunk bed," said Violet. "And there's another room down the hall for you and Julie."

"Great!" said Mark, as they all walked into the house.

"I get the top bunk!" said Davis, running ahead.

"No!" said Emily. "I do!"

Mark dropped his bags on the living room floor and collapsed on the couch.

"Can you take the bags to the room?" asked Julie.

"Later," said Mark. "I'm tired."

Trixie thought he sounded a little grouchy.

"Well, I'm tired, too," said Julie.

Trixie thought Julie sounded grouchy, too.

"Oh dear," said Violet. "It was a long drive, wasn't it?"

"The kids were bickering the whole time," said Mark.

"And the traffic was really heavy," said Julie, sitting down next to Mark and putting her head in her hands.

"Well, can I get you something to eat? Or drink?" asked Violet.

From the bedroom down the hall, Trixie could hear Davis and Emily still fighting over who got to sleep in which bunk bed.

Violet didn't know what to do. It was usually so quiet at the house. Now, however, with so many people there, there was a lot more noise. Also, everyone seemed a bit grumpy.

Trixie wasn't sure what to do, either. Then she realized that she might not have much time to patrol the neighborhood and look out for Miseries. She'd have to ask Bear and Luna to take over for a while.

Bear and Luna were two dogs who lived close by. They were Trixie's students, and they often visited Trixie's back yard. They had learned dog magic from her. Dogs had to learn how to do magic, just like humans have to learn math or spelling or cooking.

Bear and Luna were both younger than Trixie. Bear was only one year old, and still a puppy. However, Bear was already much bigger than Trixie. And he would grow even bigger! Bear was a Labradoodle (pronounced "la-bruh-doo-dl"), which meant he was part Poodle and part Labrador Retriever. He had long floppy ears and a long tail that he wagged all the time. His fur was completely black and very soft. Because he was still a puppy, Bear needed a lot of practice for his magic spells. Sometimes his spells went wrong, but Trixie had noticed that he had a particular talent for spells involving water. Maybe it was because Bear loved water so much! If there was a pond, pool, or even a puddle nearby, Bear would probably be playing in it.

Luna was a border collie. She was one year old, too. Luna was larger than Trixie but about the same size as Bear. She was very intelligent and a very hard worker. She had brown and white fur and bright brown eyes. Luna had lots of energy. She could run very fast and jump very high. She was really good at catching balls and other toys. Luna was very talkative, too. She liked barking. Luna reminded Trixie of her puppies when they were younger because Luna was so curious. Luna showed a lot of promise in being a very skilled magic user.

There was still a lot of commotion in the house. The children were still arguing and their parents were complaining about the trip. Violet was busy trying to make sure everyone got settled. Trixie realized it was the perfect time to sneak out to give some instructions to Bear and Luna. Besides, she could use a break from all the noise and fuss.

Trixie trotted out her dog door and to the backyard. There, she gave three barks. But these barks were not just ordinary barks. These were special magical barks called the Spell of Calling. When Trixie barked this way, the sound would travel directly to the ears of Bear and Luna. It was a way to get Bear and Luna to come and meet Trixie. Even though dogs already had very good hearing, the Spell of Calling could travel much farther.

Trixie cast the spell and told Bear and Luna to meet at Trixie's doghouse in Violet's back yard. This was their special meeting place. Trixie kept her spell book in her doghouse and many of her potions. Also, the doghouse is where Trixie taught Bear and Luna their magic lessons and helped them practice their spells.

After barking, Trixie walked over to her doghouse to wait for them. There was an extra skip in her step because Trixie was quite happy because of the visiting kids.

From the outside, Trixie's doghouse looked like an ordinary doghouse. It had a big front door and a roof with shingles. However, Trixie used her magic to make the inside much larger than the outside. Trixie's doghouse not only had a nice big comfy bedroom, it also had a spacious library with hundreds of books in it. Many of them were magic spell books. In the doghouse there was also a laboratory filled with glass jars and vials for making magical potions. There were shelves of magical ingredients, too.

Trixie's doghouse was the official meeting place where her students learned magic.

Bear arrived first, carrying a tennis ball in his mouth.

"Come in, Bear," said Trixie. "Why'd you bring that old tennis ball?"

Bear dropped the ball by his feet. "I didn't want to lose it," said Bear.

Luna arrived a few minutes later. "I got here as fast as I could," she said. "I had a very important bone to chew on."

"Very well," said Trixie. "Let's go inside. I've called you here for a special reason."

They went inside the magic doghouse. Trixie led them to the sitting room, where there were many rugs and pillows for sitting and lying down in comfort. Trixie was about to explain that Violet's grandchildren were visiting. She was going to ask Bear and Luna to watch out for Miseries while she spent time with the kids. She didn't want the Miseries spoiling their visit.

But before she could explain, Luna interrupted, "I already know why you called us here."

"Yeah, me too," said Bear.

"You do?" asked Trixie in surprise.

"Oh yeah," said Luna, wrinkling her nose. "It stinks around here. There must be Miseries nearby."

"Yuck," said Bear. "It smells like a dead bird covered in spicy mustard and rotten chocolate sauce."

Luna put her snout in the air and sniffed. "To me it smells like a stale pickle buried under a stink bush."

Some people think that dogs like the smell of garbage and other yucky things. However, dogs don't like bad smells any more than you or I. They only sniff and snuffle at icky smells to find Miseries. All Miseries smelled disgusting.

Miseries not only spread misery and were miserable themselves, they smelled miserable. That was the best way to know if a Misery was nearby. Their terrible smell.

But Trixie was shocked at what Bear and Luna said. "You smell Miseries? Here?" she asked.

"Yeah," said Luna, wrinkling her nose. "I could smell them a block away."

Trixie took a deep breath. She smelled it, too! Misery stink! "Oh, dog bones!" she groaned. "I hadn't noticed. My sense of smell must be really getting bad!"

Bear sniffed the air. "Must be at least a couple by the smell of it."

"Oh, this won't do at all!" cried Trixie. "If the Miseries find Emily and Davis they'll make them feel miserable and grouchy and sad! Then they'll never want to come visit again!"

Chapter Three

Bear and Luna sat up and looked at Trixie.

"What should we do?" ask Luna. "We're happy to help."

"Thank you," said Trixie. "First, we need to figure out where the Miseries are lurking and what they are doing. Then we must get rid of them."

"They can't be far, judging by the smell," said Bear. "When I find them, I'll— I'll—" Bear didn't finish his sentence. "Mrs. Trixie, what should I do when I find them?"

"We'll figure it out," said Trixie. "I have just the spell."

Trixie put on her eyeglasses and went into the library. She tilted her head to see through her glasses.

She looked at the books on the shelves. When she found just the right book, she took it gently in her jaws and pulled it from the shelf. Then she used her nose to flip through the pages.

"Ah, there it is," said Trixie. "It's called the 'Eyes that See' spell. This will save us some time because it will allow us to see the Miseries in addition to smelling them. Luna, grab my cauldron."

A cauldron is a large, iron cooking pot that could be used to make things like stew or soup. But it could also be used to make magic spells.

Luna brought the cauldron to Trixie.

"Now for the ingredients," said Trixie. "Can both of you help fetch them from the shelves?"

"Sure," said Luna and Bear.

"Thank you," said Trixie, looking at the spell book. "For this potion, I need three owl eyelashes, two carrot seeds, and a shard of broken glass."

Luna searched among the cupboards. There were many small bottles and jars with hand-written labels. After a minute or two, they brought Trixie the proper ingredients. Then Trixie read further in the recipe and asked them to get more ingredients.

Trixie blinked her eyes three times and a small fire started under the cauldron. As Bear and Luna poured the ingredients into the cauldron, Trixie climbed up on some nearby pillows and held a large spoon between her paws to stir the mixture.

When everything was added, the mixture bubbled and boiled and glowed an eerie blue color.

Trixie ladled the potion into three small dog bowls. "As soon as this cools, we can all drink it, and we'll be able to see Miseries for the next twelve hours."

When the potion was cool, they all lapped it up.

"Mm," said Luna. "It tastes like dessert!"

"It tastes like the color blue!" said Bear.

Trixie smiled at the younger dogs, but she actually didn't like the potion's flavor very much.

"How will we know it's working?" asked Luna.

"It's working," said Trixie. "As soon as you drink it, it starts working. Now we just have to look for Miseries. Follow your nose, and keep your eyes open."

"You two search the neighborhood," said Trixie. "I'll join you in a few minutes. I'm just going to pop into the house and check on my human and her grandkids. Then we can search around the neighborhood."

"Okay!" said the younger dogs.

They left Trixie's backyard and began searching the neighborhood. Trixie went inside to look around. She hoped everyone wasn't so grouchy anymore. But when she got to the living room, the first thing she saw was Davis sitting on the couch playing a game on a tablet, and right beside him was a Misery!

The Misery had an evil looking smile and was poking and pinching Davis. The boy, of course, couldn't see the Misery, and couldn't really even feel what the Misery was doing. Instead, Davis shifted uncomfortably and scowled. The Misery was making him feel miserable!

Trixie lowered her brow in a scowl and growled. Then she charged at the Misery, barking at it.

"Rowf, rowf, rowf!" barked Trixie.

Trixie's barking startled the Misery and it floated away from Davis.

It's working! thought Trixie. Now if only she could chase the Misery outside, then she and the other dogs could use some more magic to get rid of it completely.

"Trixie!" said Davis. "Quit barking at me. It's annoying!"

Trixie kept barking. The Misery backed away, closer to the door. Trixie had almost chased the Misery out the front door, but just then, Violet, Mark, and Julie walked into the living room. They were all frowning and looking unhappy.

Trixie glanced over. *Oh no!* thought Trixie.

The humans all had Miseries surrounding them. There were Miseries everywhere!

But before Trixie could react, Violet said, "Why is Trixie barking so much? The last thing we need is more noise."

The Miseries were hissing in Violet's ear and pulling at her hair. Trixie knew the Miseries were probably telling her awful things to make her think she didn't want her family to visit anymore. This is how the Miseries worked. They told the humans lies. They said unkind things to the humans.

This made the humans miserable because they believed the lies the Miseries told them. The humans thought these things were their own ideas. This could make the humans feel sad, angry, or lonely.

Trixie wanted most of all to chase the Miseries away from Violet. She turned to Violet and began barking at the Miseries.

"Woof! Woof! Woof woof woof!" she barked.

"You need to go out, Trixie," said Violet. She tried to capture Trixie, but Trixie ran between Violet's legs.

Trixie barked at the Miseries. She nipped at them and chased them. A couple of them got frightened and left the room. Trixie ran around the room and nipped and barked at the other Miseries. She knocked over a lamp.

"Trixie!" shouted Violet. "Come here! You have to go outside!"

To avoid Violet again, Trixie ran underneath a side-table. She bumped the table and a few picture frames fell onto the floor.

"Trixie!" Violet shouted again. "Stop your naughty behavior!"

Trixie barked and barked, but there were too many Miseries. When there were lots of Miseries together, they had more courage. They hissed at Trixie and laughed at her. She ran after them again, but her paws slipped on the hardwood floor. She went sliding across the room and got tangled up in Julie's feet. Julie tripped and tipped over a potted plant. There were broken things everywhere, and everyone was getting annoyed with Trixie.

At last Violet came up behind Trixie and chased her out. Trixie ran through her doggy door and into the back yard again.

"Out you go!" said Violet. Her voice sounded angry.

The Miseries watched Trixie through the windows. They all laughed wickedly at her. Trixie scowled back at them. Violet never would have thrown her out like that if it weren't for the Miseries. Something had to be done!

Chapter Four

Trixie signaled for Bear and Luna again by using three barks and the Spell of Calling. The two of them trotted up to the house together.

"We didn't find any Miseries," said Bear. "We've been all around the block, and we haven't seen any. Where is all this Misery stink coming from?"

"They're inside the house!" growled Trixie.

"Oh no," said Luna. "With the grandchildren?"

"Yes," said Trixie angrily, "and they're ruining everything! Everyone in there is grouchy and annoyed!"

The dogs walked around the house and looked in through the windows.

In one room, they saw Emily trying to read a book, but two Miseries were nearby. They pinched her and hissed into her ear. Emily scowled. The dogs could see she was having trouble reading. She looked like she was in a very bad mood.

In another room, they saw Davis still sitting on the couch with the tablet. He was playing a game. But one of the Miseries that Trixie had chased away was bothering him again. Davis jabbed his fingers angrily at the game on the tablet. It wasn't going the way he wanted. He lost his temper and tossed the tablet aside.

The dogs looked in the guest room window. The curtains were mostly shut, but they could see partially in. More Miseries! They were whispering into Mark and Julie's ears, making them argue. Trixie saw other Miseries moving through the room, making sure no one was happy or content.

"Oh this is just awful!" growled Trixie. "I never thought there'd be so many Miseries in my own house."

"They probably came with the family in the car," said Bear.

"Maybe the kids were fighting during the drive," said Luna.

Trixie nodded. "That would give the Miseries plenty of power."

Bear barked. He was eager to chase the Miseries. "Well, what should we do?"

"The poor family," said Luna. "They all look so hot and angry."

"That's it!" said Trixie. "If we could just cool them down a little, maybe they wouldn't be so angry. Then they will make better choices. That will make the Miseries weaker."

"Cool them down? How?" asked Luna. "Violet doesn't even want you inside the house!"

Trixie pressed her lips together. It had been a long time since Violet had chased her out of the house. She didn't like it.

"Bear," said Trixie, "You're good with water. Perhaps we could entice the children to come out and play in the sprinklers. That might cool their anger."

Bear barked excitedly. "Oh yes! Wonderful! Perfect! I'll do it! I'll do it!"

"Well," said Trixie. "Go on, get to it,"

In the back yard, there was a hose connected to a faucet. There was a sprinkler connected to the hose. Bear took the faucet handle in his mouth and turned it, and the sprinkler came to life. It spun around and squirted water into the back yard. However, Bear and the others knew that an ordinary sprinkler might not convince the kids to come out.

And so Bear began barking. They were magical barks! He was casting a spell. Bear also ran in circles around the sprinkler.

The sprinkler now began to shoot big magical sprays of sparkling water high into the air.

Bear ran faster around the sprinkler, and the water flew higher. It flashed in the sunlight and created magical patterns.

The water hit the windows of the rooms where the kids were.

It worked!

Davis and Emily saw the sprinkler water. They pressed against the windows and watched. Then they ran to their parents and asked if they could go outside and play in the water.

Violet looked out the window and saw the sprinkler water, too. "Hm," she said. "I don't remember turning on the sprinkler. And I surely don't remember the sprinkler acting that way."

"Well done, Bear!" said Trixie.

Bear grinned and wagged his tail. His spells did not always work out. He was still learning. This time he knew he had done really well.

"This lovely cool water will help the kids settle down," said Trixie. "And then we'll have to figure something else out for the adults."

Chapter Five

Trixie, Bear, and Luna watched as Emily and Davis came out into the back yard. They'd changed into their bathing suits. They carried beach towels. They were smiling and laughing.

Bear's water spell was working great! The sprinkler was shooting jets of water high into the air. The splashing water seemed to take the shapes of fish and birds. The water droplets caught the sunlight and cast colorful patterns onto the house and grass.

"Wow!" cried Emily. "This is great!" She let the water splash her face and arms.

Davis ran around the sprinkler and got soaking wet. "Whoo whee!" he yelled.

Trixie smiled. The kids were laughing and running, and there were no Miseries in the back yard. The Miseries hadn't noticed when the kids left the house.

"It's working!" Trixie barked.

She was very relieved. It was very difficult to rescue kids from the Miseries. The sprinkler was working well. Luna and Bear barked happily.

"Good job, Bear!" cried Luna.

Bear's tail wagged like crazy. He joined the kids as they played in the water. Luna and Trixie began to play in the water, too.

Then something bad happened.

Davis was running around and letting the water rain down on him. The magical water jets seemed to really cool him down. He acted happy and relaxed. Emily was laughing and having fun, too.

But then Davis and Emily ran into one another. It was just an accident, and no one was hurt. But both of them fell onto the grass, and both of them became cross.

"Hey!" said Emily. "You knocked me down!"

"No!" replied Davis. "You got in my way!"

They began to bicker angrily.

"Oh, dear!" said Trixie. "This will attract the Miseries from inside the house!"

Trixie and the other two dogs looked at the house. Yes! A Misery inside the house heard the kids arguing. He was a big, mean-looking Misery. He came straight through the wall of the house. The nasty smell of the Miseries came with him.

The dogs began to bark at the Misery, but he was already whispering into the kids' ears. Who knows what he was saying, but it made the kids even more angry. They began pushing and shoving each other. They said unkind things to one another.

"Go back into the house!" shouted Emily. "I don't want to be around you!"

"I was here first!" yelled Davis. "You go in the house and leave me alone!"

The whole back yard was now totally miserable. And it smelled bad, too! More Miseries were coming out of the house to help the kids get more angry and miserable.

"This makes me so sad," said Trixie to Bear and Luna. "They're really such good children. This is one of the worst cases I've seen."

Luna narrowed her eyes at the Miseries. "What can we do, Trixie? It seems like there's just too many Miseries and their power over the family has grown too strong. Even sweet Violet has been affected."

"If only the humans could start making some better choices," said Bear. "Then they'd at least have a chance against the Miseries."

"Indeed," said Trixie.

Trixie knew how hard it was to make good choices every single time. It wasn't always easy to be kind and thoughtful to your siblings.

When the Miseries were around, it made everything even more difficult.

By this time, both Emily and Davis were very gloomy. Emily threw Davis's nice dry towel into the sprinkler water. Davis smeared mud on Emily's face. The Miseries were laughing wickedly and pointing at the kids. Both of the kids stomped back into the house.

"Mom!" yelled Davis. "Emily is ruining everything!"

"Dad!" shouted Emily. "Davis is being mean to me!"

"You two quit tattling and get along!" said Julie.

"Last year when the grandkids visited," said Trixie, "we all played fetch with Davis and went for walks with Mark and Julie. Emily sat on a blanket in the shade and read her book."

"This time," Luna added, "the Miseries are ruining their fun! They won't have any nice memories from this vacation!"

When Trixie heard the word "memories," she had an idea. "Luna!" she shouted. "That's it!"

"What's it?" asked Luna.

"There's another potion we can try," said Trixie.

"It's very difficult, but if you two help me, it will be very powerful!"

"What potion is it?" asked Bear.

"There's no time to explain!" Trixie replied. She ran toward the doggy door. "I've got to get back into the house and grab some things. Meet me in the doghouse in ten minutes!"

Chapter Six

After about ten minutes, the dogs had all returned to the magical doghouse. Trixie came through the door holding something in her jaws. It was a jar of cinnamon.

"What's that?" asked Bear.

"Cinnamon," said Trixie. "We're going to try to make the family remember some of their happy memories. And all good memories have a little cinnamon in them somewhere."

"Happy memories?" Luna said, frowning. "There's no way any of them will be able to think of happy memories. They're all grumpy, grouchy, angry, and annoyed! Even Violet!"

"You're right," said Trixie. "Cinnamon by itself won't do the trick. But we'll give the family a little magical help."

Trixie put on her glasses and pulled another heavy book from her bookcase. She blew a layer of dust from the book. Then she opened the book with her nose and flipped through the pages.

"Here!" said Trixie. "This is the spell we'll use."

Bear and Luna looked at the book and said, "Oooh!"

All three dogs darted around the doghouse, fetching the ingredients and dropping them into the cauldron. Trixie's magical flames glowed and crackled under the cauldron. Soon, the mixture was bubbling and steaming, filling the magical doghouse with a magical scent. And finally, Trixie added a dash of cinnamon.

Luna sniffed the air and said, "It smells like gingerbread!"

"No, to me it smells like going to the pond in the park," said Bear sniffing.

"To me," Trixie said with a smile, "it smells like marshmallows and campfire!"

"How come it smells different to each of us?" asked Bear.

"It seems to smell different to different noses," said Trixie. "But in a way, it smells the same to all of us."

"Huh?" said Luna.

Trixie smiled. "It smells like *memories!*"

"Oooh," said Luna. "So, it smells like our favorite memories?"

"Exactly," said Trixie.

"Well, any smell is better than those Miseries!" said Bear.

They all agreed. Trixie hated how stinky Violet's house had become with the stink of Miseries.

After the potion had simmered for a while, the three dogs looked into the cauldron. It was a shimmering silvery color.

The smell was wonderful!

It smelled like all their favorite memories—the smell of fresh air, the aroma of warm food on a cold day, the smell of the lawn after it's been mowed.

Trixie adjusted her glasses and read from the spell book.

Then she barked and growled in the way that the spell book had indicated and the bubbling mixture glowed more brightly.

"It's ready," said Trixie. "Now for the hard part. We

have to somehow get the potion into the house so that the people can smell it."

"How?" asked Bear. "The cauldron won't fit through the doggy door."

"He's right," said Luna. "Let's think about this. How can we get all this potion into the house?"

"Yes," said Trixie with a frown. "And it will be too suspicious if we all walk in carrying potion bottles in our mouths."

"Maybe we could wait until they're all sleeping," said Bear. "Then we can sneak inside with the potion."

Trixie made a face.

"No, that's too long to wait," she said. "The entire first day of vacation will be ruined! And they might not even be able to sleep with the Miseries making them miserable."

The three dogs thought some more about it.

It would have been a lot easier if the dogs could have just told the humans about the potion, but humans didn't fully speak the language of dogs.

"Hold on!" said Bear excitedly. He was wagging his tail so hard, it shook his whole body. "I think I have an idea!"

But before Luna or Trixie could say anything, Bear leaped into the cauldron!

Chapter Seven

If Violet's family hadn't been so bothered by the Miseries, they might have noticed the dogs coming into the house through the doggy door. If Violet's family hadn't been so busy quarreling with each other, they might have noticed that the dogs were dripping wet!

But Violet's family didn't notice when the dogs came in. They didn't notice that the dogs were wet with a strange, silvery liquid. The humans were all in sour moods. They were all too distracted by the Miseries to notice anything. The Miseries were whispering in their ears to keep them all miserable.

"I want to go home!" said Davis.

"Go to your room, Davis," said Julie.

"My room is at home!" said Davis.

"Then go to some other room!" said Mark.

"Stop fighting, all of you!" shouted Violet.

Trixie came up and stood quietly beside Violet's chair.

Bear walked slowly over to the couch, where Emily and Davis were sitting.

Luna walked over and stood between Mark and Julie.

"Who let all these dogs in here?" asked Julie. "Look, they're all wet from the sprinklers."

When the dogs were in place, Trixie barked, "Now!"

All three dogs began shaking themselves.

You've seen dogs do this before. When they get wet, they shake themselves to get dry. Drops of water go flying everywhere. If you are unlucky enough to be near a wet dog, you will definitely get wet when dogs shake themselves.

But these dogs weren't wet with water, they were wet with magic potion. Little drops of it sprayed everywhere. It didn't stain the carpet or damage the furniture. It just spread everywhere, and then it seemed to vanish.

In fact, the humans didn't notice the dogs at all,

until the dogs started shaking their fur and sending droplets of silvery liquid all around them.

"Argh! They're getting us all wet!" said Mark, holding up his hands.

"Stop, dogs, stop!" cried Violet. "We're all getting wet!"

The dogs smiled; this was exactly what they had hoped for.

"Keep shaking!" Bear barked.

The dogs shook and shook. Sparkling magic potion was flying through the air.

"Go outside, dogs!" shouted Violet, shooing them toward the door.

The dogs ran through the doggy door and into the back yard. Then they went to the living room window to see what would happen next.

"What now?" asked Luna.

"Now we wait," said Trixie.

"I don't think it's working," said Bear. "They look just as grumpy and upset as ever."

"And there are Miseries all over the place!" cried Luna.

"Patience," said Trixie.

But it was true. Everyone in the whole family looked irritated and cross. They frowned and scowled. The Miseries around them had grown huge, they were taking up almost the whole room. The Miseries jeered and cackled.

Then Emily got up from the couch. Something across the room caught her eye. Emily went to the bookshelf and picked up a book. Then she opened the book and smelled it. Emily loved the way books smell.

"Oh, I love this book," said Emily. "I started reading it last year!"

Violet joined Emily and looked at the book. "That's right! You couldn't wait to see if the mermaid defeated the sea witch."

"Look!" said Luna. "Those Miseries suddenly got much smaller!"

"It's working!" said Trixie.

Davis looked like he was remembering something, too. "I smell the leather of my baseball and baseball glove!" He ran to the car to get the ball and glove.

"I smell molasses cookies," said Mark. Three Miseries were jabbing him and hissing into his ear, but Mark looked a little less cross. "Hey, Mom, are you baking molasses cookies?"

"No," said Violet, "but we can bake some if you want."

"Oh," said Julie. "Yes, let's make cookies like we did last time we visited!"

"Look at those two Miseries!" cried Bear. "They're growing skinny and small!"

All through the house, the Miseries were having a terrible time. Some of them got shorter and shorter until they were barely as tall as Trixie.

Some of them grew so thin they could barely be seen. All of the Miseries seemed to be getting tired. Many of them began to leave, floating away like shreds of old spider web.

Davis came back into the house with a baseball and his baseball glove.

"Hey, Sis!" he said. "Do you want to play catch? You can use my glove."

"Okay," said Emily. "But I want to finish this book later."

"You kids go play outside," said Violet. "The grown-ups are going to make cookies. Then, when they're done, we can have cookies and play a game together."

"Thanks, Grandma!" said Davis. He and his sister went into the back yard together.

The dogs were amazed to see the last of the Miseries shrink down to practically nothing.

"But the Miseries are still there," said Luna. "They haven't all gone away."

"No," said Trixie. "A few will sometimes hang around. But now that everyone is choosing to be kind and polite, the Miseries have almost no power. The Favorite Memories potion has made them feel happier and less grumpy."

"So, when the humans are being kind and happy," said Luna, "the Miseries can't bother them so much?"

"Exactly," said Trixie.

And so the dogs watched over the family. Slowly, they all became less grumpy. The kids played catch for a while. Then Davis played in the sprinkler while Emily read her book. After that, they all played a board game and had cookies and milk.

"I'm sorry I was so grouchy before," said Julie.

"Me, too!" said Mark.

"Yes," said Violet, "We were all acting grouchy. What happened?"

"It was like a bunch of grumpy ghosts came in to haunt us!" said Emily.

The humans all laughed at this, but the dogs only looked at each other. They knew that's what really happened.

Trixie breathed a sigh of relief. She had finally defeated the Miseries. Trixie was upset that she had let so many Miseries get inside her house. However, she was proud that she and her students were able to chase most of them away.

"Thank you, Luna," she said. "Thank you, Bear. I couldn't have done it without you."

"You're welcome!" they said.

Bear and Luna returned to their homes, but later that evening they returned. Together, the dogs peeked through the windows again. The family had lasagna for dinner. The kids helped set the table. Mark held Violet's chair when she sat down.

"This is delicious!" said Julie.

"Yes," Emily agreed. "It's yummy!"

Mark and Davis cleared the table and washed the dishes. Then the family went on a walk together. When they returned home, they watched a little TV and read books. Then they went to bed.

The dogs squinted through the windows. There were no Miseries in sight. Not even little ones.

"Where'd all the Miseries go?" asked Bear.

"They're gone!" said Trixie. "Violet and the family were able to drive them all away." Trixie wagged her tail happily. "At last! Now we can all enjoy their visit."

Bear and Luna promised to keep a watch over the neighborhood for the next few days to make sure no Miseries came back. They wanted Trixie to enjoy her time with her visiting family.

Trixie knew that they'd do a good job. They were good students. Trixie went back inside through her doggy door. There was a different feel in the house now. It was peaceful and relaxing. Trixie took a deep breath.

And it doesn't stink anymore! she thought. Then she went upstairs, curled up in her doggy bed, and fell fast asleep.

Please leave a review

Thank you for reading this book. I hope you enjoyed it! I would really appreciate it if you would please take a moment to review Pet Magic: Trixie's Special Guests at the retail site where it was purchased. This helps me to reach new readers. Thank you!

—A.M. Luzzader

WWW.AMLUZZADER.COM

- blog
- freebies
- newsletter
- contact info

About the Author

A.M. Luzzader is an award-winning children's book author who writes chapter books and middle grade books. She specializes in writing books for preteens including *A Mermaid in Middle Grade and Arthur Blackwood's Scary Stories for Kids who Like Scary Stories*

A.M. decided she wanted to write fun stories for kids when she was still a kid herself. By the time she was in fourth grade, she was already writing short stories. In fifth grade, she bought a typewriter at a garage sale to put her words into print, and in sixth grade she added illustrations.

Now that she has decided what she wants to be when she grows up, A.M. writes books for kids full time. She was selected as the Writer of the Year in 2019-2020 by the League of Utah Writers.

A.M. is the mother of a 12-year-old and a 15-year-old who often inspire her stories. She lives with her husband and children in northern Utah. She is a devout cat person and avid reader.

A.M. Luzzader's books are appropriate for ages 5-12. Her chapter books are intended for kindergarten to third grade, and her middle grade books are for third grade through sixth grade. Find out more about A.M., sign up to receive her newsletter, and get special offers at her website: www.amluzzader.com.

facebook.com/a.m.luzzader
instagram.com/amluzzader

About the Illustrator

Illustrator Joshua Bostwick's love of drawing began at a young age, when he spent hours drawing all sorts of animals and doodling cartoons.

After receiving a bachelors degree in art at Utah State University, Josh moved to Salt Lake City, where he now lives with his wife and four children. In addition to illustrating children's books, Josh also contributes to comic books, designs corporate logos, and works on fine-art projects. His favorite things to draw are narwhals and sloths.

When he's not illustrating books, Josh enjoys collecting action figures and sharing 80s and 90s movies with his kids.

Follow Josh on social media at www.instagram.com/joshuabostwick2525. You can find more information about Josh by visiting his portfolio at www.behance.net/joshuabostwickart or e-mailing him at Justjoshinart@gmail.com.

instagram.com/joshuabostwick2525

OTHER BOOKS BY
A.M. Luzzader

Pet Magic

For ages
6-10

OTHER BOOKS BY
A.M. Luzzader

Decker's Video Game Rescue Agency

For ages 6-10

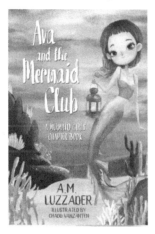 

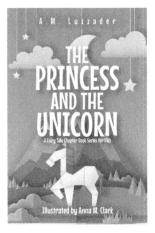 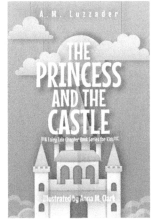

OTHER BOOKS BY
A.M. Luzzader

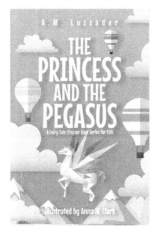

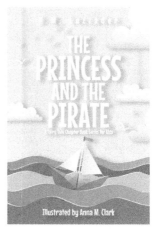

A Fairy Tale Chapter Book Series for Kids

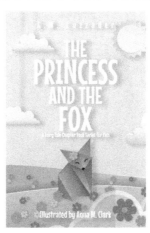

For ages
6-10

OTHER BOOKS BY
A.M. Luzzader

Magic School for Girls

For ages
6-10

Arthur Blackwood's Scary Stories for Kids

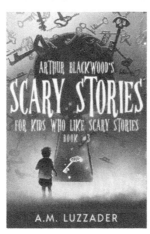

For ages 8-12

OTHER BOOKS BY
A.M. Luzzader

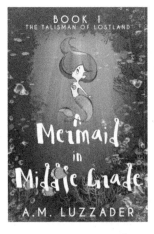 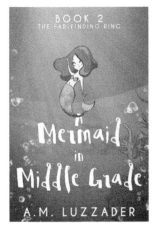

A Mermaid in Middle Grade
Books 1-3

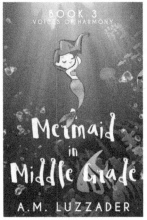

For ages
8-12

OTHER BOOKS BY
A.M. Luzzader

Hannah Saves the World
Books 1-3

For ages
8-12

Made in the USA
Columbia, SC
13 November 2023

26172813R10055